# THE PEOPLE SHALL CONTINUE

## 40TH ANNIVERSARY SPECIAL EDITION

BY SIMON J. ORTIZ • ILLUSTRATED BY SHAROL GRAVES

Children's Book Press, *an imprint of* Lee & Low Books
New York

Many, many years ago, all things came to be.
The stars, rocks, plants, rivers, animals.
Mountains, sun, moon, birds, all things.
And the People were born.
Some say, "From the ocean."
Some say, "From a hollow log."
Some say, "From an opening in the ground."
Some say, "From the mountains."
And the People came to live
in the Northern Mountains and on the Plains,
in the Western Hills and on the Seacoasts,
in the Southern Deserts and in the Canyons,
in the Eastern Woodlands and on the Piedmonts.

Some people fished, others were hunters.
Some people farmed, others were artisans.
Their leaders were those who served the People.
Their healers were those who cared for the People.
Their hunters were those who provided for the People.
Their warriors were those who protected the People.
The teachers and the elders of the People
all taught this important knowledge:

"The Earth is the source of all life.
She gives birth.
Her children continue the life of the Earth.
The People must be responsible to her.
This is the way that all life continues."

The People of the many Nations visited
each other's lands.
The People from the North brought elk meat.
The People from the West gave them fish.
The People from the South brought corn.
The People from the East gave them hides.
When there were arguments,
their leaders would say,

"Let us respect each other.
We will bring you corn and baskets.
You will bring us meat and flint knives.
That way we will live a peaceful life.
We must respect each other, and the animals,
the plants, the land, the universe.
We have much to learn from all the Nations."

Nevertheless, life was always hard.

At times, corn did not grow and there was famine.

At times, winters were very cold and there was hardship.

At times, the winds blew hot and rivers dried.

At times, the People grew uneasy among themselves.

The learned men and women talked with each other

about what to do for their People,

but it was always hard.

They had to have great patience

and they told their People,

"We should not ever take anything for granted.

In order for our life to continue,

we must struggle very hard for it."

But one day, something unusual began to happen.

Maybe there was a small change in the wind.

Maybe there was a shift in the stars.

Maybe it was a dream that someone dreamed.

Maybe it was the strange behavior of an animal.

The People thought and remembered,

    "A long time ago, there were men

    who came upon the ocean to the Western Coasts."

The People thought and remembered,

    "A long time ago, there were red-haired men

    who came upon the ocean to the Eastern Coasts."

But these visitors had not stayed for long.

They met with some of the People

and soon they left upon the ocean for their homes.

But now, the People began to hear fearful stories.

Strange men had arrived on the shores of the South.
Spanish, these men called themselves.
They came seeking treasures and slaves.
These men caused destruction among the People.
The Nations of the South were burned
by heedless and forceful men.

Soon, there were other dreadful stories.

More men, these with their wives and children,
arrived on the Eastern Coasts.
English, French, Dutch, they called themselves.
They spoke with a fervor that frightened
the People who met with them.
They taught about a God whom all should obey.
They said they were special men of this God.

Soon, the People saw the destruction
of their Nations.
They soon found out it was the aim
of the English, French, and Dutch to take their lands.
The rich and the powerful of these men
formed an American government.
They wanted the land because
it was fertile with forests and farmland
and wealthy with precious minerals.
And they wanted the People to serve them as slaves.

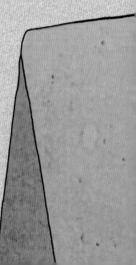

When the People saw these men did not respect them and the land, they said,
   "We must fight to protect ourselves and the land."
In the West, Popé called warriors from the Pueblo and Apache Nations.
In the East, Tecumseh gathered the Shawnee and the Nations of the
Great Lakes, the Appalachians, and the Ohio Valley to fight for their People.
In the Midwest, Black Hawk fought to save the Sauk and Fox Nation.
In the Great Plains, Crazy Horse led the Sioux in the struggle to keep their land.
Osceola in the Southeast, Geronimo in the Southwest, Chief Joseph in the
Northwest, Sitting Bull, Captain Jack, all were warriors.

They were warriors who resisted and fought
to keep the American colonial power from taking their lands.

From the 1500s to the late years of the 1800s,
the People fought for their lives and lands.
In battle after battle, they fought until they grew weak
Their food supplies were gone, and their warriors were killed or imprisoned.
And then the People began to settle
for agreements with the American government.

The leaders of the People agreed to Treaties.

The People said they would stop their armed fight.

The Americans promised the People

they could live on land they both agreed

was the People's land.

Upon this land, the People could hunt

and fish and have their sacred ceremonies.

Upon this land, the Nations of the People could live.

The People thought,

     "The Earth is the source of all life."

They knew they must have the courage to continue.

The People promised to honor the Treaties.


The People had to agree to live on reservations.

Much of the reservation land was very poor.

There were no more buffalo to hunt

and the deer and elk were scarce.

Many of the People ran away

and they were forced back by the Americans.

The Nations of the People were weakened.

They were broken in united strength.

Soon, more Americans came.
They were gold miners, railroad men,
outlaws, missionaries, ranchers.
They wanted the rest of the land the People had.
Treaties were broken by them
and the reservations grew even smaller.

The Americans sent government agents.
They told the People they could not live
the way they had before.
The missionaries asked the government
to put a stop to the sacred ceremonies,
the dances, and the songs of the People.

The government agents gathered the children.
They took the children to boarding schools
far from their homes and families.
The children from the West
were taken to the East.
The children from the East
were taken to the West.
The People's children were scattered
like leaves torn from a tree.
At schools far from home,
the children were taught to become Americans.
They learned to be ashamed of their People.

The People went to schools.
They went to Christian churches.
They served in the American army.
Some even almost became Americans.
But they were still the People.
They farmed and raised livestock.
They made and sold crafts for a living.
Nevertheless, the People were very poor.
There were no jobs on the reservations.
Even though they didn't want to,
many of the People had to leave.

They were moved by the government
into the cities across America.
Oakland, Cleveland, Chicago, Dallas,
Denver, Phoenix, Los Angeles.
They worked in factories, on railroads,
in businesses, even for the government.
Often they were discouraged
and their families suffered in the cities.
They struggled hard for their lives.

All this time, the People remembered.

Parents told their children,

    "You are Shawnee. You are Lakota.

    You are Pima. You are Acoma.

    You are Tlingit. You are Mohawk.

    You are all these Nations of the People."

The People told each other,

    "This is the life of our People.

    These are the stories and these are the songs.

    This is our heritage."

And the children listened.

    "This has been the struggle of our People.

    We have suffered but we have endured," the parents said.

    "Listen," they said, and they sang the songs.

    "Listen," they said, and they told the stories.

    "Listen," they said, "this is the way our People live."

All across America,

the Nations of the People were talking.

The Cheyennes in the cities and the Navajos in the country.

The Seminoles in Los Angeles and the Cherokees in Oklahoma.

The Chippewa in Red Lake and the Sioux in Denver.

Everywhere, the People on the reservations,

in small towns, in the large cities—

they were talking, and they were listening.

They were listening to the words

of the elder People who were speaking.

> "This is the life that includes you.
> This is the land that is yours.
> All these things that were pushed away from us
> and broken by the American powers and government,
> they are alive, and we must keep them alive.
> All these things will help us to continue."

Once again, the People realized

what was happening to the land.

They realized it was the powerful forces

of the rich and the government

that made the People suffer.

The People looked around them
and they saw Black People, Latino People,
Asian People, many White People and others
who were kept poor by American wealth and power.
The People saw that these People
who were not rich and powerful shared
a common life with them.
The People realized they must share
their history with them.

"We shall tell you of our struggles," they said.
"We are all the People of this land.
We were created out of the forces
of earth and sky, the stars and water.
We must make sure that the balance of the Earth be kept.
There is no other way.
We must struggle for our lives.
We must take great care with each other.
We must share our concern with each other.
Nothing is separate from us.
We are all one body of People.
We must struggle to share our human lives with each other.
We must fight against those forces
which will take our humanity from us.
We must ensure that life continues.
We must be responsible to that life.
With that humanity and the strength
which comes from our shared responsibility
for this life, the People shall continue."

## AUTHOR'S NOTE

Originally published in 1977, *The People Shall Continue* is a story of Indigenous peoples of the Americas, specifically in the US, as they continue to try to live on lands they have known to be their traditional homelands from time immemorial. Even though the prairies, mountains, valleys, deserts, river bottomlands, forests, sea shores and coastal regions, and swamps and other wetlands across the nation are not as vast as they used to be, all of the land is still considered to be the sacred, sovereign homeland of the People.

And despite attempts by non-Indigenous colonial forces to eradicate traditional customs, rituals, and lifestyles, these essential Indigenous practices continue to take place today. Indigenous languages are still spoken, although constant modern-day social, cultural, and economic changes have resulted in some loss of more traditional knowledge. Indigenous identity is still deeply felt by the heart and soul of the People. Traditional prayers, songs, dances, and ceremonies are communally regarded as essential, and tribal elders urge that traditions must always be continued.

Of course, many Indigenous peoples now live in US cities across the nation as urban residents amid the national citizenry of many different ethnic and cultural peoples. Indigenous peoples are a part of the struggle to achieve fulfilling lives. Like other peoples of the United States, Indigenous peoples are seeking an adequate and suitable education, and the knowledge and skills needed to secure a sustainable living. This is one of the many constant struggles that Indigenous peoples continue to face.

The Standing Rock tribal community of Sioux peoples in North Dakota have also been dealing with a great struggle. They have been fighting to stop the Dakota Access Pipeline (DAPL), because severe pollution, contamination, and devastation of land, water, air, plant life, animal life, and human life take place when oil pipelines break.

The Sioux peoples wish to protect their own health and lives, as well as the lives of everyone and everything negatively affected by heedless technological developments. The lives and lands of Sioux peoples are threatened and endangered, but so are other peoples and lands across the US and around the world. This is why the courageous call of "NO DAPL" was taken up by many other tribal Indigenous Americans as well as non-Indigenous peoples in the US, and people in Asia, Europe, South America, and elsewhere. It is not only Indigenous peoples who are sustained by and tied to the lands: we all are.

Without any doubt, the endeavor to continue to live as Indigenous Americans is sincere and serious. It is a way of living that engenders love, care, responsibility, and obligation. It must be exercised and expressed as belief, commitment, and assertion of one's humanity in relationship to others and all life beings in Creation, in order that the People shall always continue.

—Simon J. Ortiz, also known as Hihdruutsi of the Eagle Clan or People and child of the Antelope Clan or People of Acoma

Text copyright © 1988, 1977 by Simon J. Ortiz
Author's Note copyright © 2017 by Simon J. Ortiz
Illustrations copyright © 2017, 1977 by Lee & Low Books Inc.

Children's Book Press, an imprint of LEE & LOW BOOKS Inc., 95 Madison Avenue, New York, NY 10016
leeandlow.com
Book redesign by David and Susan Neuhaus/NeuStudio
Book production by The Kids at Our House
The text is set in ITC Legacy Sans
The illustrations are rendered in pencil and ink, then digitally enhanced
Manufactured in China by Jade Productions
15  14  13  12  11  10  9  8
First Edition

Library of Congress Cataloging-in-Publication Data
Names: Ortiz, Simon J., 1941–author. | Graves, Sharol, illustrator.
Title: The people shall continue / by Simon Ortiz; illustrated by Sharol Graves.
Description: Revised edition. | New York: Children's Book Press,
an imprint of Lee & Low Books, 2017.
Identifiers: LCCN 2017017146 | ISBN 9780892391257 (paperback: alkaline paper)
Subjects:  LCSH: Indians of North America—History—Juvenile literature.
Classification: LCC E77.4 .O77 2017 | DDC 970.004/97—dc23
LC record available at https://lccn.loc.gov/2017017146